The Adventures of

LITTLE MISS CRAZY HAIR

The Girl with Curl

Written by Christopher & Alejandro Garcia-Halenar

Special Thanks to:

- Rey & Regan for allowing us to use Vivian as our muse - C.G-H. & A.G-H.

- Our team of 'Little Editors' who had a BIG impact: Hazel, Ezra, Vivienne, Sarai, Emma, Reeni, Finn, Xander, Hudson, Eva, Charlie, Sam, Gabriella, Maddie, and Sarah - C.G-H. & A.G-H.

ISBN-13: 978-1-7326044-0-7
Illustrations by: Sophia Jin

Published by:
XanMaxBooks
www.xanmaxbooks.com

Printed in the United States.

To Vivian,
whose radiant curls
are only surpassed
by her beautiful mind

A Note from the Authors

Little Miss Crazy Hair was written for our curly headed niece, Vivian, on her fifth birthday. Being five can be a terrifying time for a kid - leaving the world of kindergarten and entering the domain of first grade. There's a lot to be anxious about: new school, new teacher, new friends. Five-year-olds (and most adults we know) just want to fit in. The last thing they want is to be different because of the curl of their hair, the color of their eyes, the pigment of their skin, their height, their weight, the way they dress- the list goes on.

Little Miss Crazy Hair gives positive recognition to the value of being unique and celebrates Vivian's beautiful, curly hair. The message of this book is that not looking like everyone else doesn't make you odd, it makes you special.

After receiving a less than enthusiastic response from five-year-old Vivian (c'mon, not many five-year-olds get excited about receiving a book on their birthday), the book went on a shelf and was never released for distribution.

In this revised edition, "being unique makes us special" is still the main message of the book, but we have added a new dimension. We are pleased to introduce Little Miss Crazy Hair's 7 BEEs.

The 7 BEEs are embedded in the illustrations and not called out in the book narrative. Each of the BEEs highlight an attribute that reflects Little Miss Crazy Hair's daily adventures. The 7 BEEs are by no means all-inclusive. Entire libraries could be dedicated to attributes of being a better person. But the 7 BEEs are representative of the adventures of Little Miss Crazy Hair in these pages.

Discussion of each BEE, and its pertinence to individuals, is purposefully left open. Some may be timelier and result in a hearty conversation, while others may need very little discussion. The decision is left to the reader and the child.

Not all-inclusive, but a good starting point.

Enjoy.

Chris & Alex

Little Miss Crazy Hair's 7 BEEs

BEE Polite

BEE Determined

BEE Brave

BEE Kind

BEE Yourself

BEE Adventurous

BEE Grateful

This girl is a rare gem,
with none like her
She is unique,
one of a kind.
What makes her so special?

She's the girl with amazing locks of

BENDING, CURLING,

roller-coaster-turning,

COILING,

Spinning,

Out-of-control twisting,

stand-on-your-head,

GLORIOUS,

MAGICAL CURLS.

She is

Little Miss Crazy Hair

Every morning, she and her best friend Duke
make the first big, important decision of the day...

How will Little Miss Crazy Hair wear her extraordinary, magical hair?

When Little Miss Crazy Hair wakes...
Duke is waiting for her.
"How will you wear your hair today?"
Little Miss Crazy Hair smiles big and wide.
"Today I feel EXTRA SPECIAL,
I will be a princess!
I'm going to wear my hair in a French braid!"

Little Miss Crazy Hair crowns herself PRINCESS FOR THE DAY.
She prepares her royal high tea.
With her best manners, she asks, "Lord Duke, would you like cream AND sugar in your tea?"
Licking his lips, Duke howls, "Oh boooooyy! Yes, both, please!"

On Tuesday morning,
Duke licks Little Miss Crazy Hair awake,
tickling her cheek.
"How will you wear your hair today?"
Wiping Duke's wet kisses off, she says with a giggle,
"Oh Duke, I feel like dancing!
Today, I'm going to be a prima ballerina!
I'm going to wear my hair high up on my head in a bun."

BEE DETERMINED

With tutus primped and fluffed,
Little Miss Crazy Hair and Duke stand in front of the mirror and bend,
and stretch,
and twirl.
They practice over and over,
jumping and twirling
to get their dance JUST RIGHT.

It's still dark outside when Duke wakes on Wednesday morning.

He nudges **Little Miss Crazy Hair** until she opens her eyes.

"How will you wear your hair today?"

She stretches her arms wide in a humongous body yawn.

"Oh Duke! I had the most magnificent dream!

I was Cleopatra, Queen of Egypt!

Today, I'm going to string oodles of beads and bangles in my hair!

Little Miss Crazy Hair and Duke sail their royal ship down the Nile River.
They see the dark shape of a crocodile in the water.
Duke covers his eyes and trembles.
"Yikes! I'm afraid of crocodiles! They EAT little dogs like me!"

Little Miss Crazy Hair jumps to the front of the boat and shouts,
"Mr. Crocodile, MOVE OUT OF THE WAY!"
The crocodile bows, dipping his nose in the water.
"All hail Little Miss Crazy Hair!"
He swims away and Duke cheers for Little Miss Crazy Hair !

Duke is still snoring when Little Miss Crazy Hair bounces out of bed on Thursday.
"Wake up, Duke! Today, I'm going to wear my hair in a ponytail!"
Duke rubs his paws over his eyes. "Hmmm? A ponytail? Why?"
"I'm going to be a veterinarian, every animal's best friend!"
Duke dances in excitement.
"That's an idea I can get my paws around! Can I be your nurse?"

Little Miss Crazy Hair treats her toy family with tender loving care.
She hands out apple juice medicine and gumdrop pills.
"You must be a really good veterinarian. Look at that line!" says Nurse Duke.

On Friday, Duke finds Little Miss Crazy Hair eating her breakfast.
"How will you wear your hair today?"

Little Miss Crazy Hair is dizzy with excitement!
"I'm feeling extra adventurous. I want to be a jungle explorer!
Today, I am going to wear my hair loose and natural."

Creeping ever so softly, Little Miss Crazy Hair sneaks up on Duke.
Like a jungle cat, she leaps into action.
"ROOOOAAAARRRR!!!"
Duke jumps into the air, his tail between his legs.
"You scared the b-b-b-bark out of me. I thought you were going to b-b-b-bite me!"
"Oh Duke, you're my very best friend. I would never hurt you."
Hand in paw, they explore the deep, dark jungle together.

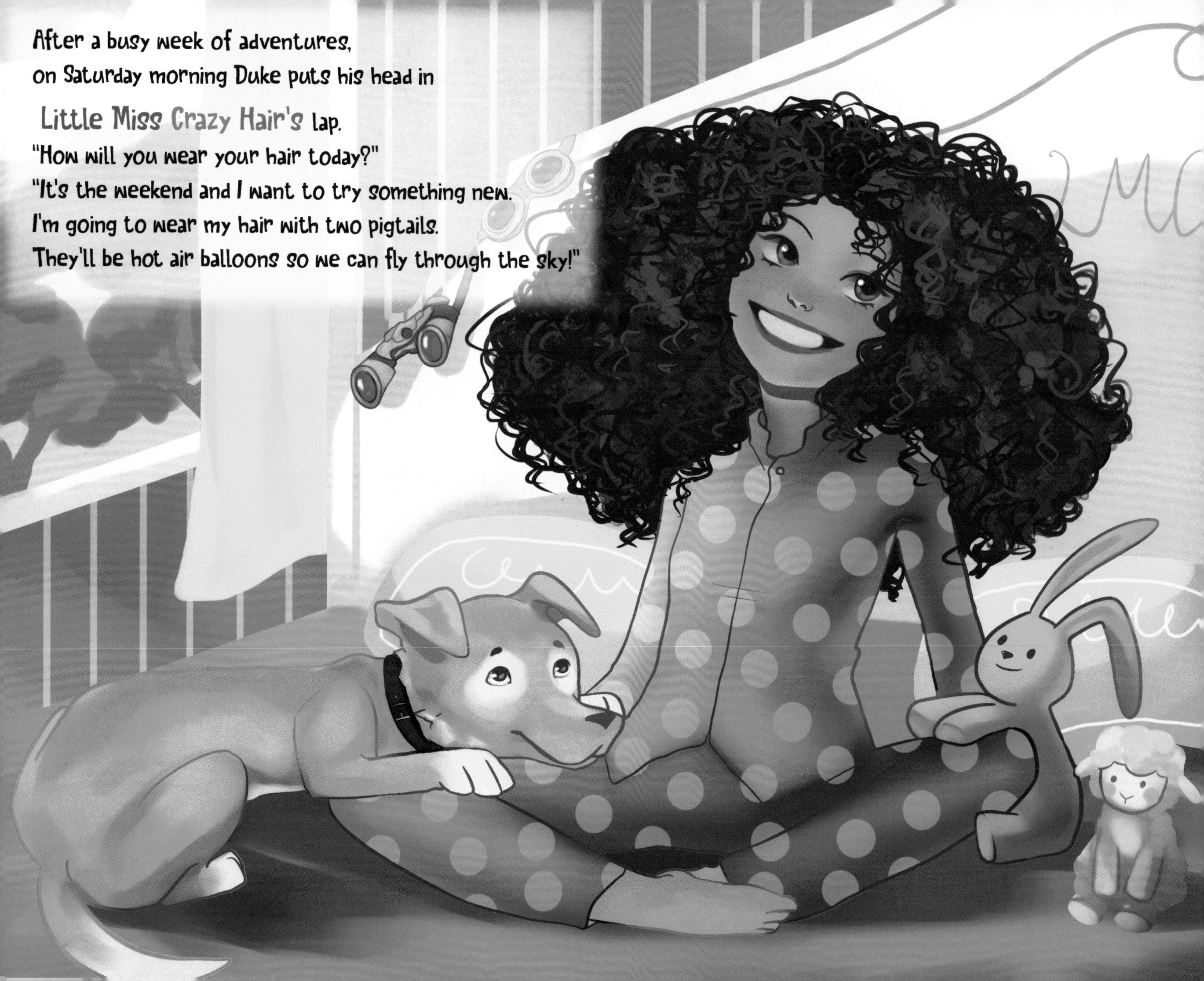
After a busy week of adventures,
on Saturday morning Duke puts his head in
Little Miss Crazy Hair's lap.
"How will you wear your hair today?"
"It's the weekend and I want to try something new.
I'm going to wear my hair with two pigtails.
They'll be hot air balloons so we can fly through the sky!"

Duke jumps on Little Miss Crazy Hair's back and they fly above the clouds.
They soar so high they can see their house,
their neighborhood,
their school,
and the whole city.

All is quiet on Sunday morning when Duke nuzzles Little Miss Crazy Hair awake.
"How will you wear your hair today?"
Slowly, she opens her eyes
and pulls back the sheets.
"Come here, boy. Let's cuddle."
As fast as a jack rabbit, Duke hops into bed.
He and Little Miss Crazy Hair snuggle tight.

BEE GRATEFUL
In the blink of an eye, they're both asleep, full of smiles.
They dream of all their adventures,
Little Miss Crazy Hair and her amazing locks of
BENDING, CURLING,
roller-coaster-turning,
COILING,
spinning,
out-of-control twisting,
stand-on -your-head,
GLORIOUS,
MAGICAL CURLS.

About the Authors

Chris and Alex Garcia-Halenar are the loving and doting uncles of their niece, Vivian, who inspired this book with her spunk, her smarts, and of course, her fabulous hair. They are firm believers that every child is unique and should be celebrated.

Chris and Alex and their two sons, Xander and Max, live in in the land of sunshine, dreams and hurricanes called South Florida where they enjoy each with equal measure.

Additional works include the award-winning children's book, Xander's Story, which tells how their dream of having a son became a reality through the gift of surrogacy.

About the Illustrator

Sophia Jin is a young artist, born in China, who now lives in the majestic country of New Zealand. Her love for art and creating beautiful things started when she was very small. Over the years she self-taught herself to draw and create wonderful pieces of art.

Sophia credits most of her inspiration from surrealistic art, things with a unique flair, and the overwhelming support and encouragement of her parents and family.

At the time of illustration of this book, Sophia is a high school student with the passion and desire to continue her talent in making art and design as her full-time career.

CPSIA information can be obtained at www.ICGtesting.com
Printed in the USA
BVIW121344240619
551818BV00007B/32